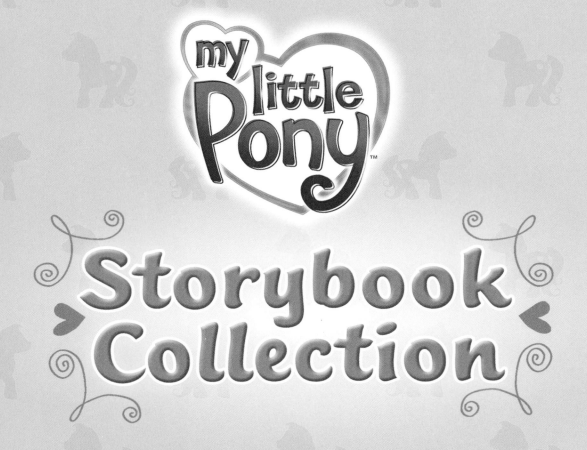

my little Pony™

Storybook Collection

Stories by
Ann Marie Capalija, Kate Egan,
Jodi Huelin, and Namrata Tripathi

Illustrations by
Ken Edwards, Lyn Fletcher,
and Carlo LoRaso

Table of Contents

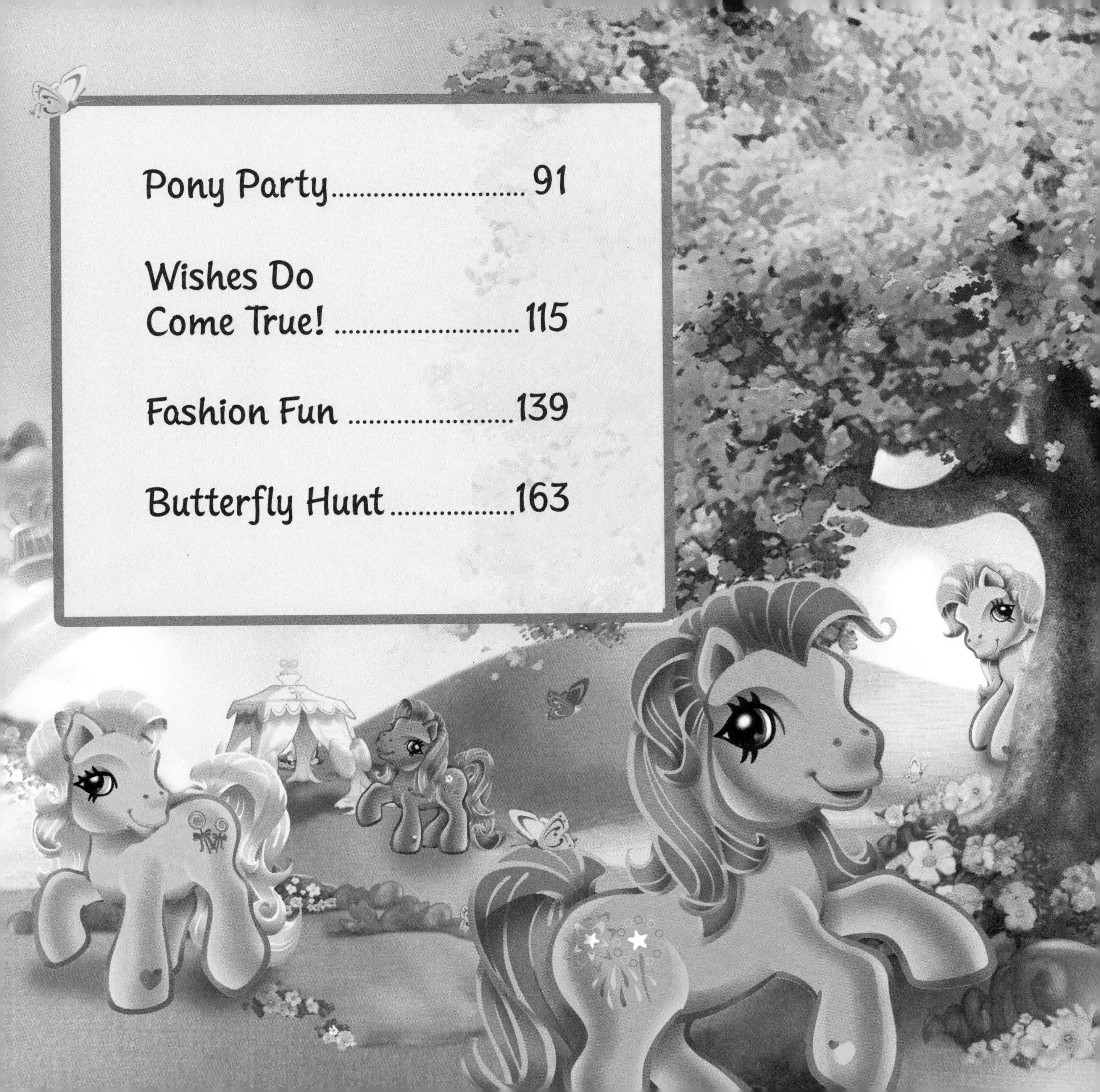

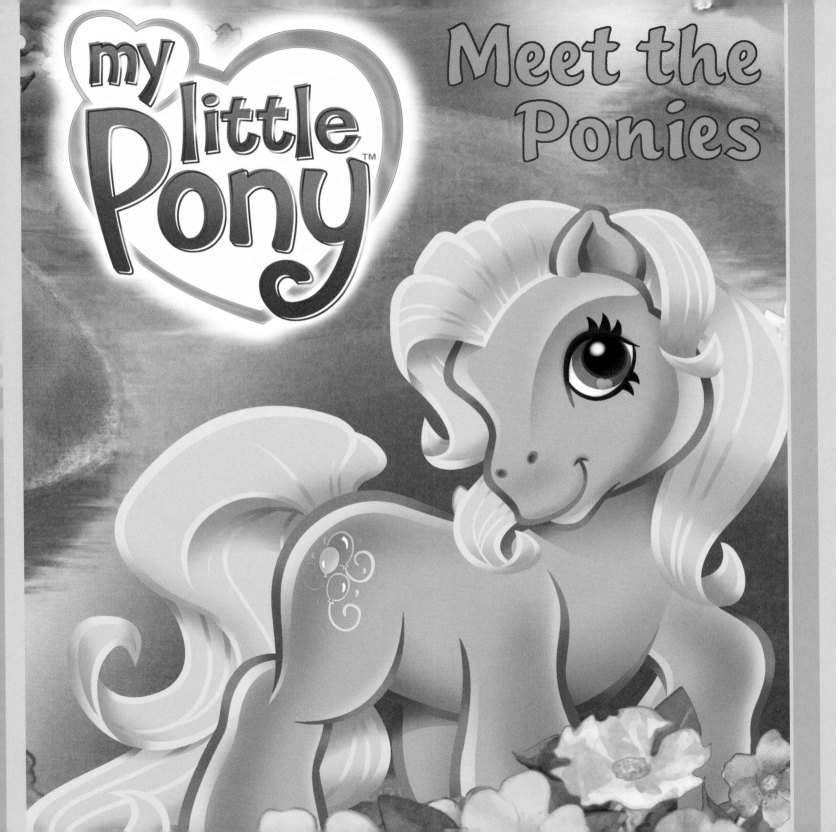

Sweetberry

Sweetberry will make you
a cake or a sundae.
It doesn't matter
if it's Tuesday or Monday.
She loves to make things,
especially sweets.
She often comes up
with the yummiest treats.
Her creations don't always
turn out quite right,
but when they do,
they are out-of-sight!

Cutie Mark

Sparkleworks knows
you can always be more,
if you only let
your imagination soar.
She says if you set
your mind on something new,
there isn't a thing
that you can't do.
She thinks challenges
are a lot of fun,
since they bring out the best
in everyone.

Cutie Mark

Minty

Minty sees things
from her own point of view.
In everything old,
she brings out the new.
Her friends say her logic
is a bit upside down,
but she'll make you smile
when you're wearing a frown.
She has a mint green body
and pink-and-white locks.
She loves to collect things—
especially socks!

Cutie Mark

Kimono

Kimono is a pony
who is very wise.
Each story she tells
holds a special surprise.
She may be serious
for most of the day,
but this quiet pony
still loves to play.
Hopscotch is
her favorite game.
Visit her—
she'll be glad you came!

Cutie Mark

Sunny Daze

When you meet Sunny Daze,
you'll know right away—
you've made a friend
that loves to play.
She'll invent a game
you've never seen,
where you can be
a princess or a queen.
She loves performing tricks
and having fun.
She's bursting with energy,
like the shining sun.

Cutie Mark

Rainbow Dash

Rainbow Dash loves
to ride on rainbows.
She's an adventurous pony,
as everyone knows.
She always believes
that bigger is better.
She'll try anything
if only you let her.
If she hasn't done it,
it's never been done—
that's what makes Rainbow Dash
so much fun!

Cutie Mark

Pinkie Pie

You'll know Pinkie Pie
by her pink-and-white hair.
If you need a friend,
she'll always be there.
This little pony
is as curious as can be.
Hear all her questions
and you're sure to agree.
She's always asking,
"How?" "Why?" and "Who?"
But you'll make her jump
if you shout, "Boo!"

Cutie Mark

My Little Pony

Pinkie Pie's Spooky Dream

It was a perfect night in Ponyville.
The sky was clear. The air smelled sweet.
Millions of stars twinkled high above.

"Let's sleep outside tonight!" said Sparkleworks.
"That's a great idea," said Rainbow Dash.
"Count me in!" Pinkie Pie added.

So the ponies gathered their coziest blankets,
and headed out to find the perfect spot.

They settled down on a nice grassy meadow
with a view of the stars.

"Let's tell spooky stories!" suggested Rainbow Dash.
"S-s-spooky?" asked Pinkie Pie.

"One night, long, long ago, there was a pony with pretty,
pink hair," Rainbow Dash started.
"Like me?" asked Pinkie Pie.
"Exactly like you," said Rainbow Dash.

"The pony was on her way to the Castle,
but there was a terrible storm," Rainbow Dash continued.
"It was very dark, so she used the moon as a guide.
But then, big, thick clouds covered the moon.

The pony walked and walked,
but never found the Castle.
She was lost in the woods,
and no pony ever heard from her again."

"Never?" asked Pinkie Pie.
"Never ever," answered Rainbow Dash. "But sometimes the wind sounds like her voice calling, `Woo, wooooo.'"

"I hope that there isn't a storm tonight," Pinkie Pie said.
Sparkleworks smiled. "Don't worry, Pinkie Pie," she said.
"It's just an old pony story. I've heard it a million times."

It was late, so the ponies lay down to sleep.
Sparkleworks and Rainbow Dash drifted off right away.
But not Pinkie Pie.
She kept thinking about the story.

As she looked up at the stars,
Pinkie Pie thought about that pony with the pink hair.
Could she still be out there, lost?
Pinkie Pie wondered.

Eventually Pinkie Pie fell asleep,
but unlike Sparkleworks and Rainbow Dash,
Pinkie Pie did not sleep well.
She had a terrible dream.

In Pinkie Pie's dream,
the night was cloudy.
She was walking to the Castle
when rain started to pour from the sky.

Pinkie Pie used the moon to guide her—
until a cloud blocked the moon.
"I can't see anything!" Pinkie Pie exclaimed.

She kept walking and walking,
but she couldn't find the Castle.
"I'm lost!" cried Pinkie Pie. "Lost! Lost! Lost!"

Pinkie Pie wasn't just talking in her dream.
She was calling out in her sleep,
and she woke her friends up.

"Pinkie Pie, wake up!" Sparkleworks said.
"You're having a bad dream," Rainbow Dash added.
Pinkie Pie woke up, startled.

"I was lost," Pinkie Pie said.
"Lost?" asked Rainbow Dash.
"No. You're on a sleepover under the stars
with Sparkleworks and me."

"I was trying to find the Castle, but it was dark
and I kept walking . . ." said Pinkie Pie.
Then Sparkleworks and Rainbow Dash understood.
The story Rainbow Dash told had scared Pinkie Pie.
It caused her to have a bad dream.

"That was just a story," said Sparkleworks.
"It's not real."
"She's right," Rainbow Dash said.
"I heard it a long time ago at a sleepover party."

"Dreams can seem real," Sparkleworks said.
"But they're not."
"You're our friend. We'd never let you get lost,"
said Rainbow Dash.
"Friendship is real!" said Pinkie Pie.

After the ponies went back to sleep,
they had nothing but happy dreams.
The next morning, they went to the Café for breakfast.
"Happy dreams are nice," said Pinkie Pie.
"But nothing is better than REAL, good friends!"

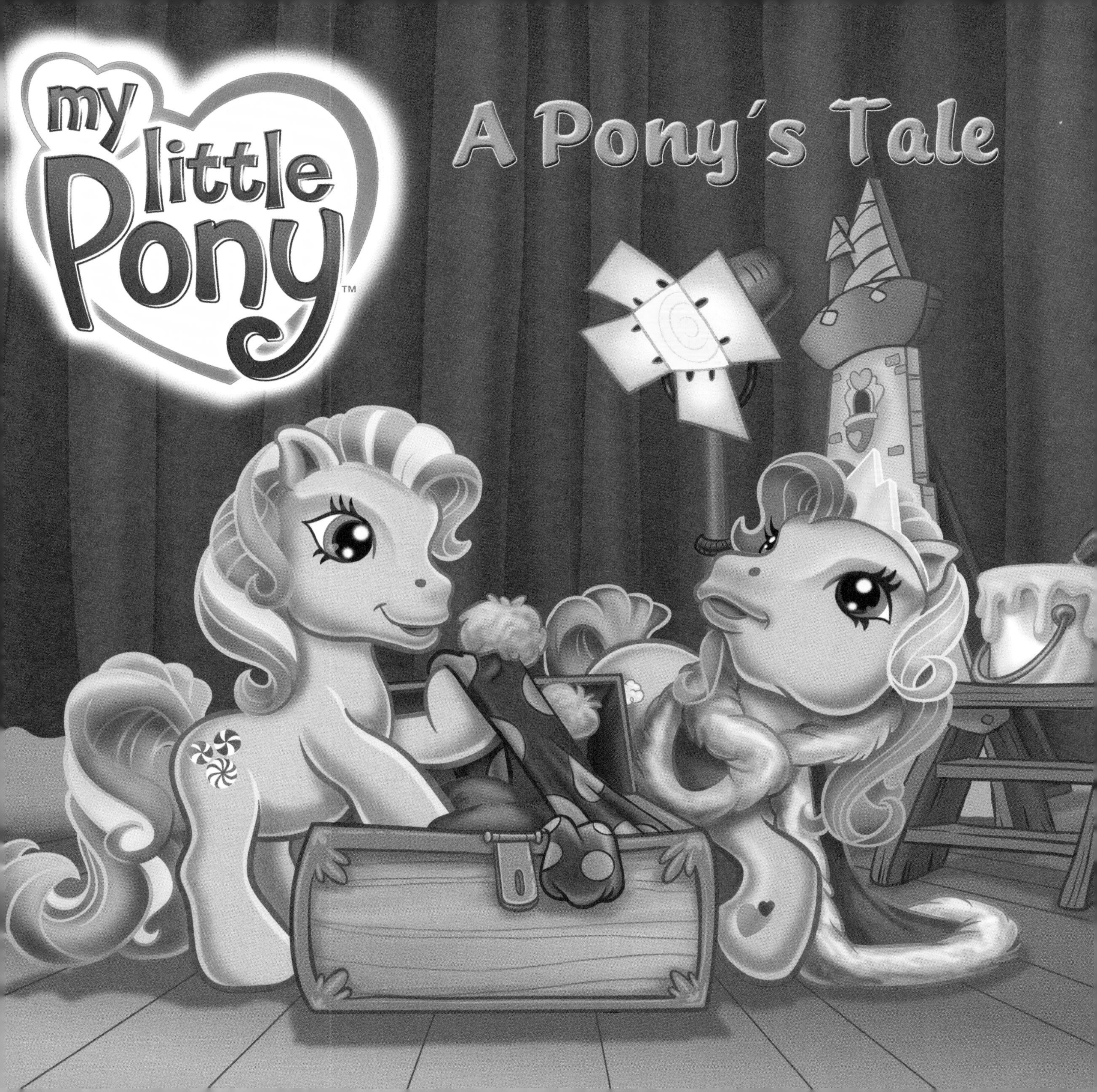
my little Pony™
A Pony´s Tale

The ponies gathered at the Castle.
Excitement was in the air.
It was the day to begin this year's Pony Play!

"I hope I get a part in the play," said Minty.
"Me, too," said Pinkie Pie.
All of the waiting was making her nervous.

"I want to play someone important," said Rainbow Dash.
Wysteria didn't want to be *in* the show.
She preferred a role behind the scenes.

Soon, all of the ponies' wishes came true.
"Look!" squealed Minty. "I get to play a clown!"
"I will play the princess!" exclaimed Rainbow Dash.

"I get to be a ballerina!" said Pinkie Pie.
Wysteria was excited. She would design
all of the sets for the play. Painting was her specialty.

Rainbow Dash.....Princess
Pinkie Pie.......Ballerin

The Crew
Cotton Candy.....Director
Wysteria......Set Desi
Kimono.......

Cotton Candy was chosen to be the director.
She was a natural storyteller.

The ponies got down to work.
They practiced every day, rain or shine.

Cotton Candy wanted the play to be perfect.
She took her job as director very seriously.
She followed the script exactly.

"Let's play a game in one of the scenes,"
suggested Sunny Daze.
"We can't," Cotton Candy said.
"That's not in the script."

"I think the princess should sit on a throne,"
said Rainbow Dash.
"No, that won't work," said Cotton Candy.
"The script says the princess should stand."

"I could tell a joke!" Minty suggested.
"Clowns are perfect joke-tellers."
Cotton Candy wasn't so sure.

Cotton Candy liked the sets, but she asked Wysteria,
"Can they be more like the ones described in the script?"

"I think Wysteria's set designs are beautiful!" said Minty.
"Me, too," added Rainbow Dash. "I wouldn't change a thing."

"If we pay perfect attention to the script,
our play will also be perfect!" Cotton Candy said.
She didn't realize that the other ponies' suggestions
might make the play even better.

With just a few days to go until the play,
Cotton Candy noticed something.

The ponies were still working hard on the play,
but they didn't seem excited about it anymore.

I should have listened to my friends, Cotton Candy realized. They all had great ideas. So what if we don't follow the script perfectly. If we add everyone's ideas, the play will be better than perfect—it will be FUN!

So Cotton Candy called a meeting.

"I want to apologize," said Cotton Candy.
"I didn't listen to your ideas because I was worried the play
wouldn't be perfect if we changed it," she said.

Cotton Candy promised that from now on,
the play would use *all* of the ponies' ideas.
The ponies were so happy.
"Hooray for Cotton Candy!" they cheered.

When the day of the play arrived, everyone was nervous.
But they needn't have worried.
Wysteria's sets were beautiful.
Princess Rainbow Dash sat on a sparkly throne.

Everyone laughed at Minty's joke,
and played along with the game that Sunny Daze invented.

"A Pony's Tale" was a wonderful success.
"Thanks to wonderful friends!" said Cotton Candy.

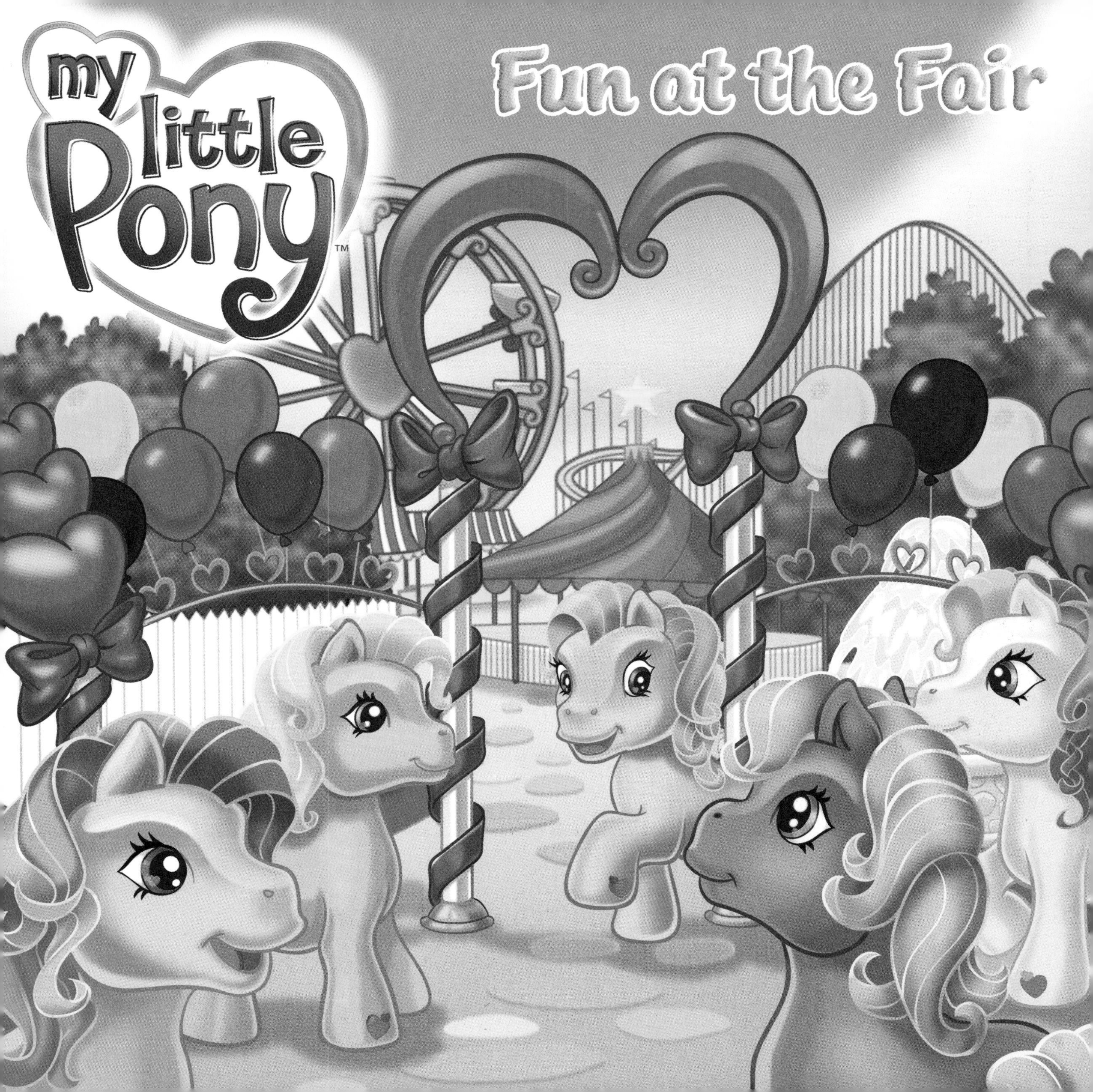
my little Pony™
Fun at the Fair

The sun was just rising over Ponyville.
The ponies were getting an early start.
They were going to a fair!

"Let's have a race!" Minty squealed.
The ponies ran through the meadow
until they reached the fair.

The friends bounded through the gate.
The fair stretched as far as they could see.

There was so much to do!

"Let's go on the bumper cars!" cried Sunny Daze.
She shared a car with Butterscotch.
They crashed into Rainbow Dash!

"Anyone want to try the water slide?" asked Wysteria.
The ponies got soaked,
but they soon dried off in the warm sun.

Butterscotch wanted a picture of all her friends.
It would remind her of their day at the fair.
The ponies crowded into a photo booth.
They made funny faces for the camera!

Then Sunny Daze said, "Let's try some games."
She leaped to a row of booths.
The ponies were ready to play!

Minty went first.
She had to jump on a platform.
If she jumped hard enough, a bell would ring.

Minty jumped with all her might.
The bell rang—Minty won!
Her prize was a cute cap.

Minty's cap was stylish, but it was not what she wanted.
She had her eye on a teddy bear!
If Minty won at three booths in a row,
she could trade in her prizes for the bear.

Minty's friends were still taking turns on the platform.
Minty headed for the next booth.
She thought of the bear. Then she tossed a water balloon.
This time she won a necklace!

Minty's friends cheered her on at the next booth.
"You can do it, Minty!" said Wysteria.
"Pony power!" shouted Sparkleworks.

The third game looked easy.
Minty just had to kick a ball through a goal.
But she didn't win with her first kick.
She didn't win with her second kick, either.

The other ponies decided to go on the Ferris wheel.
They waved to Minty from the top.
Minty was too busy to see them.

Minty missed a lot of fun.
Rainbow Dash went to the face-painting booth.
She had rainbows painted on both her cheeks.

Sunny Daze went on the roller coaster.

And Butterscotch found lots of stickers
for her scrapbooks.

Minty kept on playing,
but the ball always went in the wrong direction.
Minty still wanted to win the bear,
but she was starting to feel discouraged.

Suddenly, Wysteria was beside her.
"I'll bet you're tired," she said. "Maybe you just need a break."
The friends shared an ice-cream cone.
Then they returned to the game.

Now Minty was ready to try again.
She took a deep breath. Then she kicked the ball.
It went right into the goal.
Minty had won the third prize!

Minty traded her three prizes for the teddy bear.
She gave the bear a squeeze.
Then she gave Wysteria a squeeze, too.
A friend like Wysteria was the best prize of all!

And fireworks were the best end
to the ponies' day at the fair.

Ponyville was quiet,
but it wouldn't be quiet for long.
The ponies were having a costume party at the Castle!

Wysteria was dressed as a hula dancer.
She hung a strand of colorful flowers around her neck.
She straightened her grass skirt.
Then she rushed to the Castle to finish the decorations.

Cotton Candy frosted one last cupcake for the party.
She kept her apron tied when she was finished.
Then she put on a chef's hat.
No one would be surprised by *her* costume!

Rainbow Dash looked just like a movie star!
She smoothed her hair.
She adjusted her sunglasses.
She was ready to go.

But not all the ponies were ready.
Pinkie Pie stared at a big trunk full of dress-up clothes.
"What should I wear?" Pinkie Pie sighed.
"It's so hard to choose!"

Luckily, some of her friends were there to help.
Sparkleworks held up a tutu and twirled.
"You'd make a pretty ballerina," she suggested.
Pinkie Pie shook her head.

Sunny Daze asked, "How about a clown?"
She put a funny wig on Pinkie Pie.
Pinkie Pie couldn't see! The three friends laughed,
but Pinkie Pie still didn't have a costume.

Soon the ponies found a glittery cloak in the trunk.
And then they found a horn.
Sparkleworks had a great idea.
``Pinkie Pie, you can be a unicorn!''

Pinkie Pie loved her costume.
She couldn't wait to get to the party.

At the Castle, sparkly balloons floated in the air.
Cotton Candy was serving cupcakes.
Some ponies were already dancing.

Pinkie Pie enjoyed looking at her friends' costumes.
Kimono fluttered by with big white wings.
She made a perfect angel.

Minty was dressed as a pony from outer space.
Her outfit was shiny and silvery.
Her antennae bounced when she danced.

Everyone said they loved Pinkie Pie's costume.
She was having the best time ever.

Then someone stepped on Pinkie Pie's cloak by mistake.
Now it had a big rip near the bottom.
"No one will notice," said Rainbow Dash.
But Pinkie Pie kept sneaking peeks at the tear.

As Pinkie Pie danced, she forgot about the tear.
She also forgot to look where she was going.
Pinkie Pie danced right into the punch bowl.

Her costume was soaked and her horn broke right in half!
She didn't look like a unicorn anymore.
She wasn't having fun anymore.
She felt like crying.

Sparkleworks winked at the other ponies.
Then she waved her wand over Pinkie Pie.
"Abracadabra," she said. "Alakazam!
Bring me a costume as fast as you can!"

Minty took off her antennae.
She put them on Pinkie Pie's head.
What were Pinkie Pie's friends up to?

Rainbow Dash offered her sunglasses.
Pinkie Pie put them on.

"Doesn't she look fabulous, ponies?" Rainbow Dash asked.
Pinkie Pie pretended to smile.
She still wished she had a costume.

But Pinkie Pie's friends weren't finished.
Kimono pinned her wings on Pinkie Pie.
Wysteria handed her a bunch of flowers.
Now Pinkie Pie did look like *something*.
She just couldn't think what it was.

Sunny Daze was dressed as a cheerleader.
She jumped in the air and shook her pom-poms.
"Three cheers for Pinkie Pie!
She's a lovely butterfly!"

Pinkie Pie looked at what she was wearing.
She smiled again—this time for real.
Her new costume was beautiful.
And with friends like these, she could fly anywhere.

Twinkle Twirl's Dance Studio was a busy place.
All of the ponies were practicing for the Best Friends' Ball and
making sure their costumes were ready for the big event.

116

Serendipity was working on her superslide. Desert Rose shimmied through her salsa solo. And Starbeam was working overtime on her tap routine with master dancer and best friend Twinkle Twirl!

Besides helping her pony pals learn their dance steps,
Twinkle Twirl made sure each of her friends was ready for the ball.
They needed help with their hair, boas, capes, and necklaces.
Twinkle Twirl wanted to share something special with every pony.

Skywishes was all finished getting ready.
"Let's take a break and go fly a kite," she suggested.
"Sorry, Skywishes," replied Twinkle Twirl. "I'm just too busy today."
Skywishes knew that Twinkle Twirl wanted this year's ball
to be the best ever. Still, she decided to leave her kite outside,
just in case Twinkle Twirl changed her mind.

119

When every pony had finally left for the ball, Twinkle Twirl looked
around her dance studio and realized she had a problem.
She had loaned all her pretty things to the other ponies
and had nothing for herself to wear!

As she walked outside to go home, Twinkle Twirl saw Skywishes´ kite.
She remembered the special pony tale that said kites were wish catchers.
She whispered, "I miss my friends. I wish I were with them."

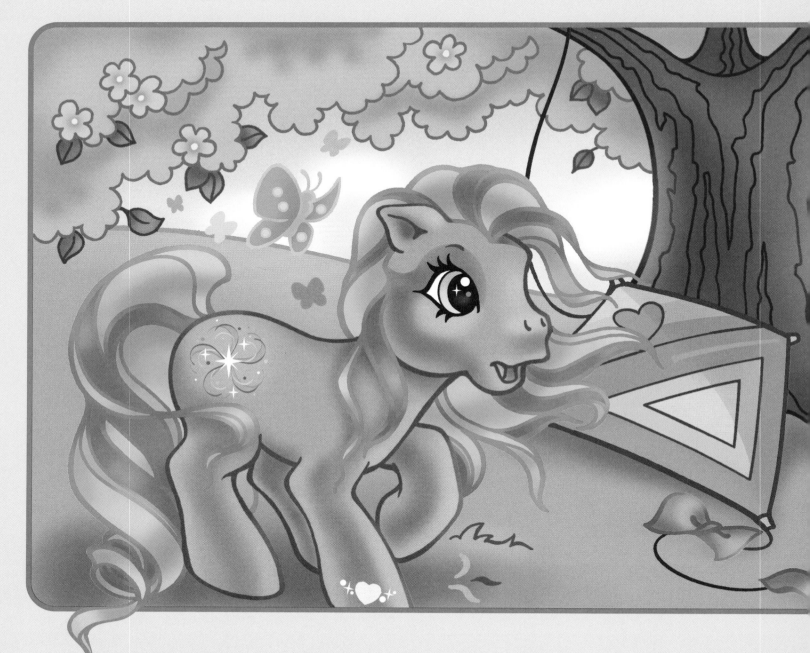

Suddenly, a mysterious and beautiful winged pony
appeared in the air.
"Consider it done," the pony said.
Twinkle Twirl couldn't believe her eyes.

"Yes, we do exist," explained Star Catcher, the smiling pegasus pony. "But the magic of the pegasus ponies will be lost forever if you tell anyone about our meeting."

Before she knew it, Twinkle Twirl was wearing
a glittering tiara and jeweled dress.
She made a grand entrance at the Best Friends´ Ball!

As all of Twinkle Twirl's friends gathered around
to admire her beautiful outfit,
she thought to herself, *My wish came true!*

The next morning, all the ponies gathered for the Best Friends' Beach Party. Everyone was excited about the sand castle tournament. They ate delicious rainbow-berry ice pops and worked on their castles.

"Three cheers for fun in the sun!" said Twinkle Twirl at the ice pop booth.
Oh, no! Chef Cotton Candy ran out of berries.
"I'll get more," volunteered Skywishes.

As Skywishes searched for more rainbow-berries,
she felt the tickle of butterflies around her head and looked up
to see a big surprise. *Could it be?*
Skywishes couldn't believe her eyes—before her was a real
pegasus pony! Skywishes ran back to her friends
to share her discovery. "I've found a pegasus pony!" she shouted.

Skywishes' friends rushed to the rainbow-berry bush,
trampling the sand castles they had spent all morning building.
But there was no pegasus pony at the berry bush.
"You shouldn't have tricked us like that, Skywishes," said Desert
Rose. Skywishes tried to explain, but the other ponies did not believe her.

Skywishes tried to regain her high spirits at the kite-flying parade. Her kite soared above the rest . . . and then was caught in a gust of wind that pulled her down to the beach.

Chasing after her favorite flyer, Skywishes ran right into
the pegasus pony she'd seen at the rainbow-berry bush.

This time she was certain her friends would believe her!
Skywishes cried out to the rest of the group. They dropped their
kites and raced over, thinking their friend was in trouble.

But when they reached Skywishes,
the pegasus pony had already flown away again.

At the marshmallow roast that night, Skywishes insisted she'd seen a pegasus pony. Twinkle Twirl believed her, but she had promised not to tell the others about Star Catcher and couldn't help Skywishes make the others believe her.

Sadly, Skywishes took her kite and ran off.
She hoped some night flying would raise her spirits. Her kite
soared high, heading toward a waterfall. Skywishes chased after
it so quickly that she ran right into the water.

Behind the waterfall, Skywishes found a sight that took her breath away. Fragrant flowers swayed in a breeze. There were rainbows everywhere, and thousands of tiny butterflies fluttered by. And best of all, pegasus ponies soared through the sky!

Skywishes was delighted by this magical place.
She explored the home of the pegasus ponies for a long time.
After a while, Skywishes was sleepy and sat down
next to a clear brook to rest.

Skywishes thought she had just closed her eyes for a moment, when she felt Twinkle Twirl shaking her awake. Opening her eyes, Skywishes wondered, *Was the land of the pegasus ponies all make-believe? Or do wishes come true after all!*

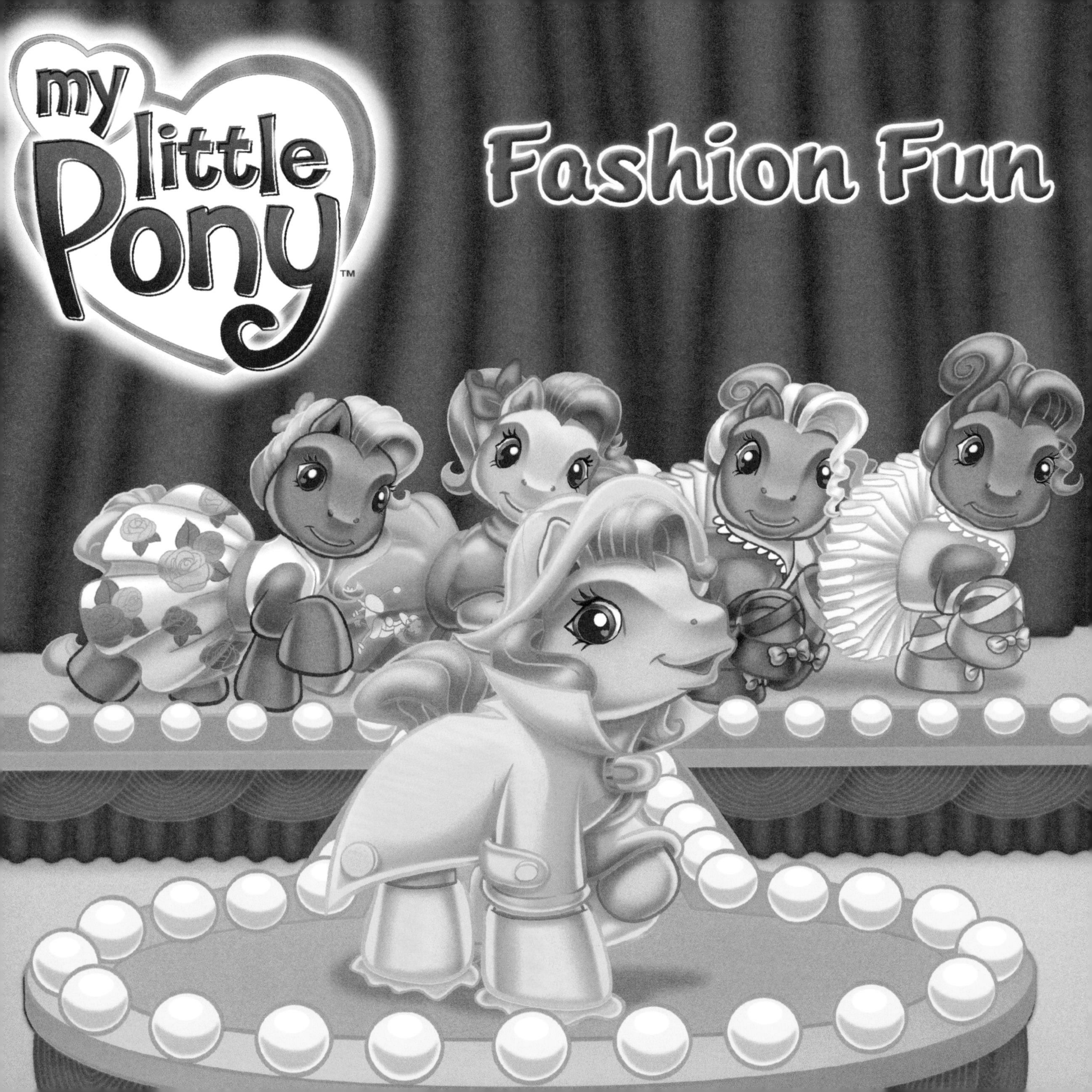
my little Pony™
Fashion Fun

Ponyville was buzzing with excitement. Sew-and-So was going to show everyone her latest designs!

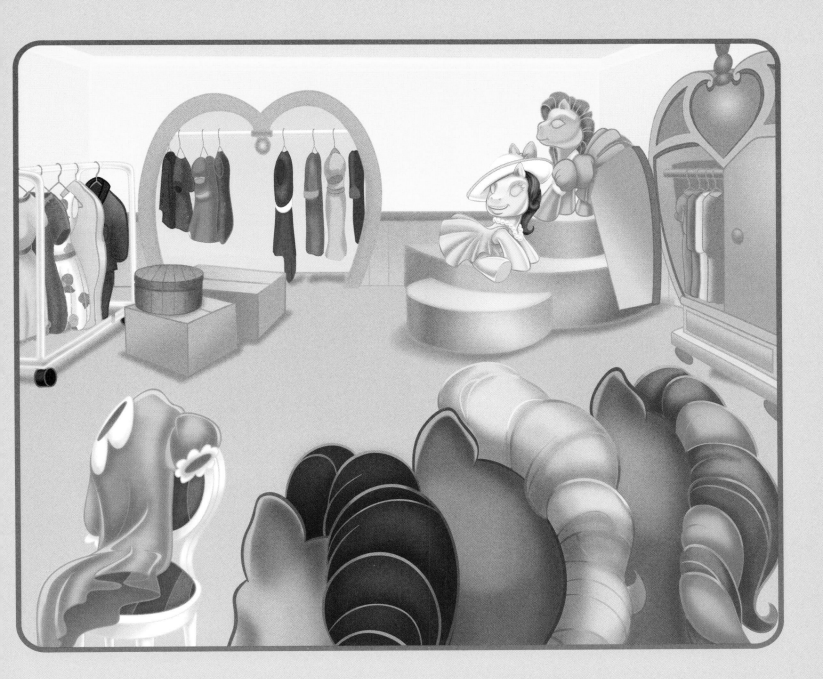

The ponies crowded into Sew-and-So's studio. New outfits and accessories were everywhere—in closets, on the backs of chairs, and even hanging from the ceiling!

"I really love this poodle dress," said Rainbow Dash.
"If I wore that I'd feel like the queen of any sock hop."

Daisy Jo admired a pretty sundress covered with colorful flowers. "These are just as pretty as the roses in my garden," she said.

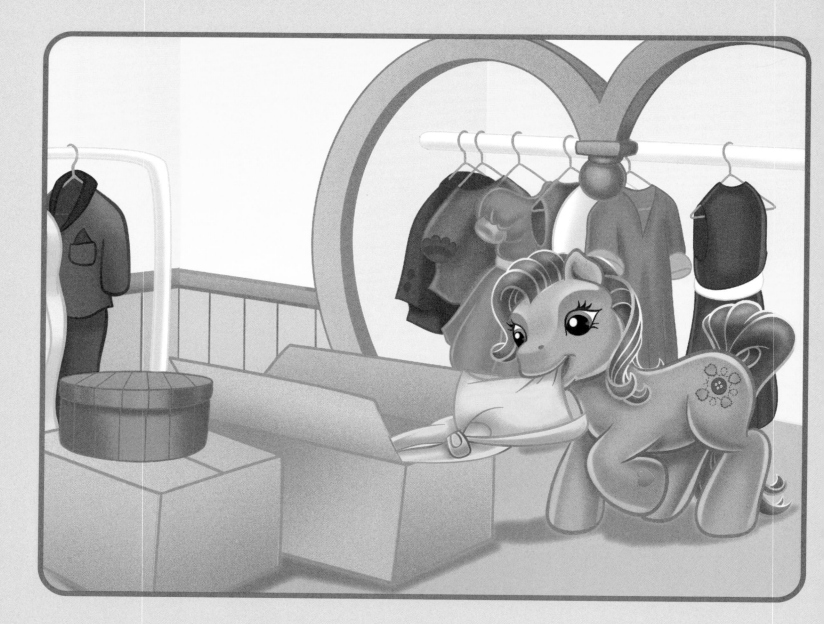

"Your roses inspired me, Daisy Jo," said Sew-and-So. "And since we all know that April showers bring May flowers, let me show you my next creation." She reached into a big box. "I'm gaga over this yellow rain slicker."

"It's perfect for any pony who wants to stay dry in style," cried Minty.

"I just thought of a great idea," said Sew-and-So.
She buttoned the rain slicker on Minty. "We should put
together a fashion show."

"Fantastic!" said Fluttershy. "I'll take the pictures."

"And I'll create a special light show," said Sparkleworks. Kimono and Wysteria offered to do the stage design. Sweetberry and Cotton Candy would cater the event. *Yum!*

All the rest of the ponies would be models in the show. They began to try on all the different outfits. Minty was so excited she raced for a yellow rain hat and tripped. *Ker-plop!*

Oh, dear. Minty was just a little bit clumsy.
What would happen to her at a fashion show?

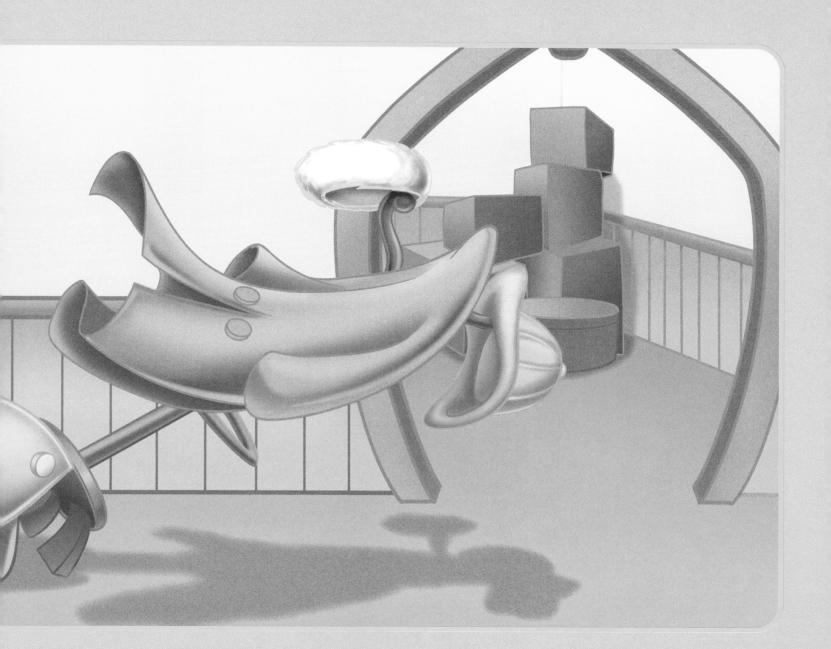

Sew-and-So saw that her friend was worried.
"You will be all right, Minty," Sew-and-So said. "We have
plenty of time to rehearse."

The ponies began preparing for the big show.
The stage crew made a long, gleaming runway.
Sparkleworks set up the spotlights.

Sweetberry and Cotton Candy whipped up some tasty treats for the audience. Rainbow Dash decorated the invitations.

Soon it was time for the dress rehearsal.
The models took their places backstage.
*I'll go last, Minty thought to herself. That way if I
make a mistake maybe no one will notice.*

"Positions, everyone," announced Sew-and-So.
The rehearsal began. Rainbow Dash danced around stage
with her skirt swishing from side to side.

Cotton Candy and Sweetberry glided onstage in frilly tutus.
Everything was going perfectly . . .

. . . until it was Minty's turn on the runway. She was more nervous than she'd ever been before. She wanted to be perfect like the other models, but halfway down the runway she slipped and fell. *Ker-plop!*

Minty got back up and kept on trying. But she kept on falling, too. The harder she tried, the harder she fell.

Minty's friends all encouraged her. "You can do it, Minty," said Sparkleworks. She knew Minty would be a great model if she could only be more confident.

On the day of the big fashion show, Sew-and-So gave Minty a
surprise gift. "I designed a little something extra to go with your
rainy-day look," she said, smiling. "These are special, rubber soled,
no-slip, wet weather, gorgeous galoshes!"

"No-slip," said Minty. "I can't wait to try them." With her new rain boots—and a special friend like Sew-and-So—Minty knew that everything would be all right.

Finally, the time came for Minty's big moment.
She walked down the runway with confidence. Her friends cheered
her on and . . . Minty stole the show!

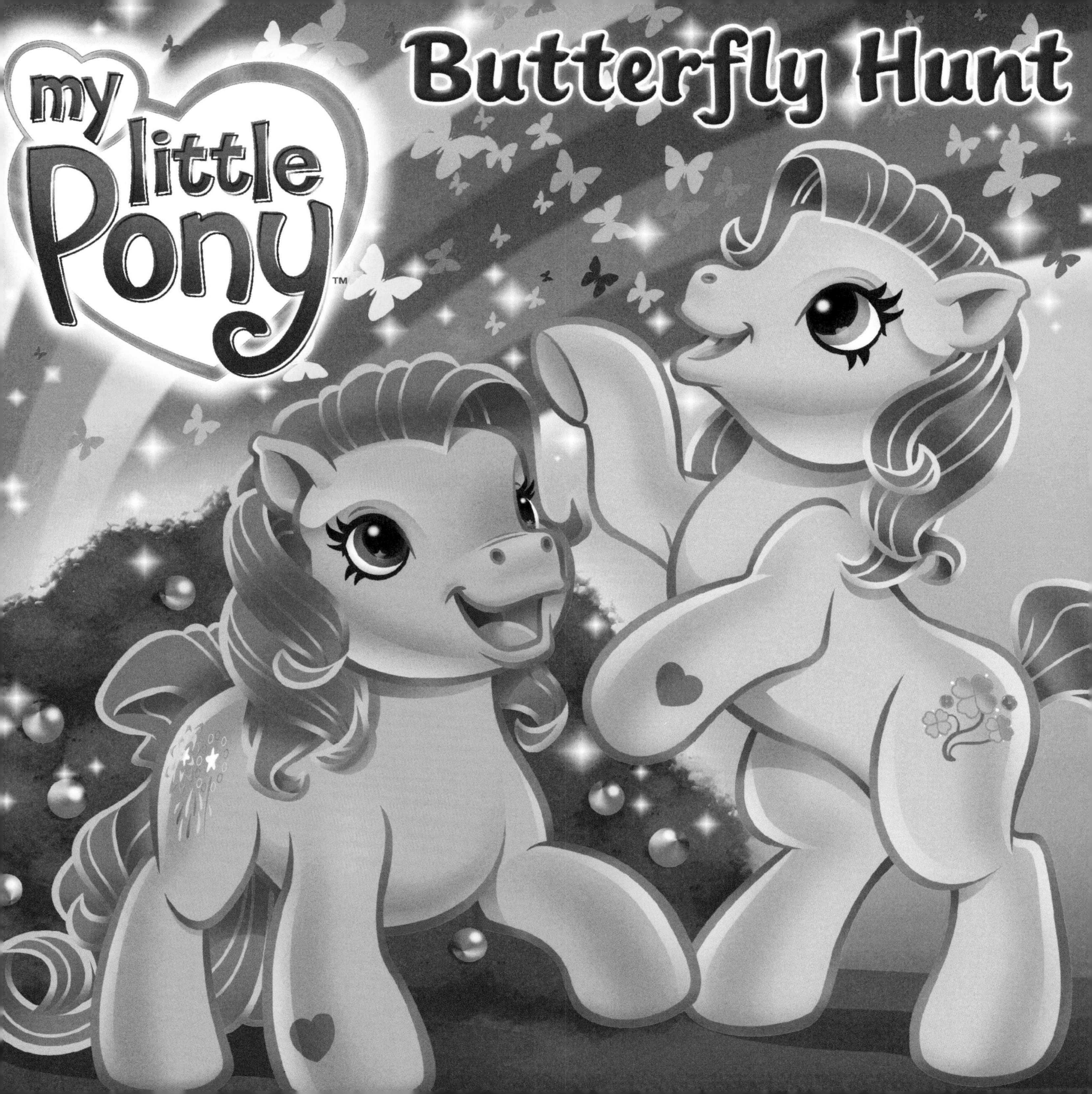
my little Pony™
Butterfly Hunt

"What a perfect day for a butterfly hunt!" said Sparkleworks.
"Thanks for inviting me, Serendipity."

"That's what friends are for," Serendipity said with a smile.

The two friends walked into the meadow side by side.
Soon a flutter caught Serendipity's eye.

Serendipity skipped off toward the stream.
Sparkleworks followed close behind.

"Look at this beauty of a butterfly!" Serendipity exclaimed.
"Those wings are almost as sparkly as your favorite
fireworks," she told Sparkleworks.

"What a lucky find, Serendipity," Sparkleworks replied.
The ponies continued on their butterfly hunt.

Soon Serendipity spotted another pretty butterfly resting on a vine of flowers. "Look at those bright polka-dot wings," said Serendipity. "Aren't they just gorgeous?"

"Wow!" said Sparkleworks. "It's as pretty as Sew-and-So's favorite dress. You sure are a lucky butterfly-finder, Serendipity."

"Butterfly hunting is thirsty work," said Sparkleworks.
"Let's stop for a drink at the wishing well."
"Great idea," replied Serendipity.

While the ponies were enjoying their deliciously cool water,
Sparkleworks saw a yellow butterfly on her tail
stretching its wings.

173

"I finally found one!" she cried out excitedly, pointing.
Serendipity looked over and spotted it.
"Oh, I see it now," she said. "It's pretty. Come on,
I'm sure we'll find more back in the meadow."

174

Sparkleworks and Serendipity walked back toward
the meadow. Sparkleworks didn't notice that the yellow
butterfly was flying after her.

After walking a ways, the two friends came to a rainbow-berry bush. "Look, Sparkleworks!" cried Serendipity. "Those are the most beautiful butterflies I've ever seen!"

Then something magical happened. The glittering group of
butterflies started flying toward the two friends.
Butterflies of every color filled the air.

"Serendipity, what's happening?" Sparkleworks asked, as she felt the butterflies lifting her off the ground.
"I don't know for sure, but I have a feeling this is going to be one amazing ride," Serendipity said. *Whoosh!*

The ponies flew higher and higher into the sky.
Sparkleworks was a little worried at first about being so
far up. But soon she began to enjoy the beautiful sights of
Ponyville below.

The butterflies carried Serendipity and Sparkleworks over the
stream and past the wishing well.

They soared above Kimono's cave, and glided past the waterfall.

Then the butterflies carried the ponies into the heart of Ponyville. They flew high above Twinkle Twirl's Dance Studio and the Cotton Candy Café. At last, the butterflies stopped above Celebration Castle, hovering in the air while Serendipity and Sparkleworks admired the view below.

Finally, it was time to come back down to earth. The butterflies gently placed the ponies on the ground. They danced in the air for a moment before flying off past the rainbow-berry bush and toward the waterfall.

"What an amazing adventure," said Sparkleworks.
"You're still the luckiest butterfly-finder ever!"

"But Sparkleworks, haven't you noticed? That little
yellow butterfly has been following you all morning,"
Serendipity said. "You found more than a butterfly—you
found a new friend!"

"A new friend?" said Sparkleworks, grinning her biggest grin.
"There's nothing luckier than that!"